Play The Harmonica Well

Advanced Instruction for the Chromatic Harmonica
but diatonic harmonica players
will learn just as much

by *Douglas Tate*

Foreword by *Larry Adler*

Cover Art - Eddie Young

Cover Scanning - Shawn Brown
Production - Ron Middlebrook

ISBN 1-57424-061-7
SAN 683-8022

© 1993 by Douglas Tate

Published by CENTERSTREAM Publishing
P.O. Box 17878 - Anaheim Hills, CA 92807

All rights for publication and distribution are reserved. No part of this book may be reproduced in any form or by any electronic or mechanical means including information storage and retrieval systems without permission in writing from the publisher, except by reviewers who may quote brief passages in review.

Foreword by ... Larry Adler

In this country you had better declare an interest. Many an MP has tried to evade that maxim and has paid for it. My interest is, I'm a fan of Douglas Tate. I respect him as a fine player, a conscientious musician and I envy him because he can so something I can't do. He can repair a mouthorgan. I, who have never mastered the principle of the hammer, can only look on in wonder. It's surprising that I don't hate him.

Also, he writes like an angel. Many a professional writer could read Tate's books on the mouthorgan and learn something about clarity, economy and style. These books should be of immense value to every mouthorganist lucky enough to encounter them.

Except me. I can read Tate's books until the cows come home ... in fact I'm waiting for one now, she's been out all night ... the fact is I'm hopelessly impractical about anything requiring manual skill. I'm writing this on a word-processor. It didn't take me long to master it. I started just after my *bar mitzvah* in 1927 and am just beginning to acquire a certain proficiency.

Doug Tate has fixed many a mouthorgan for me and they always sound better after he has worked on them. If memory doesn't fail me the way it usually does, he's even made two mouthorgans for me with stainless steel bodies (The first was stolen soon after he made it, the second was stolen out of my car recently)

What Doug Tate can't do for me I'm sure he can do for you. You're smarter than me, I can tell by looking at you. Get every one of Douglas Tate's books. You'll learn a hell of a lot from them and, if I wasn't such a klutz, I could say the same.

Play the Harmonica Well

Contents

Introduction	2	Tone Usage	24
Preamble	3	Button Movement	24
Holding	4	Trills and Turns	26
Posture	6	*Part Button Movement*	26
Mouth Position	8	*Definitions*	27
Movement	10	Projection	29
Breath Control	12	Which Hole	30
Articulation	14	Chords and Intervals	31
Phrasing	16	*Tongue Switching*	31
Sustain	17	Interpretation	32
Tone Manipulation	18	*Find the Key*	33
Vibrato	22	Useful Books and Music	34
Hand Vibrato	22	Postscript	35
Throat Vibrato	23		

Play the Harmonica Well

INTRODUCTION

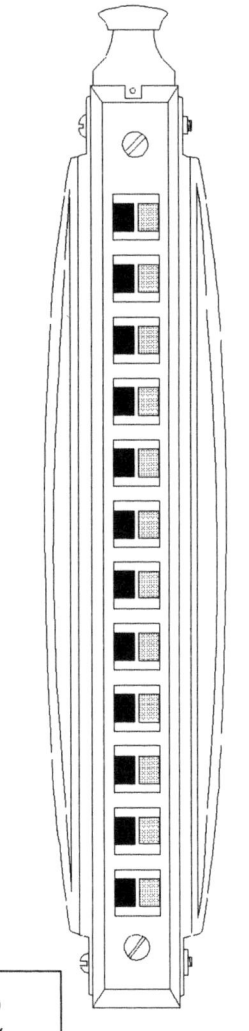

Are you really interested in improving your harmonica playing? If you are then this book is for you. In it you will find many of the fundamental musical and physical techniques for the harmonica explained in detail for the first time. This is not a book of musical exercises, that comes later!

In order for the techniques to stick, you have to work ...HARD. None of these ideas are easy to master but they will improve your playing. You will succeed only if you really try again and again to follow the instructions exactly. I have attempted to describe each technique as carefully and fully as possible. The aim has been to try and explain precisely what you are required to do in order to acquire the desired skill. Some procedures seem fairly easy but will take months (or longer!) to master. A technique is only learnt when you no longer think about it but have it as a natural part of your repertoire of 'tricks'.

The order of items in this book may seem a little odd in places. Where possible there is a logical sequence, but some techniques overlap.

I would suggest that everyone start with the sections on standing and holding. Bear with me and dig out the chunks you need.

Any book is a poor substitute for a live teacher. As there are so few harmonica teachers around so this book may be a reasonable way to either get going or to enhance your present ability.

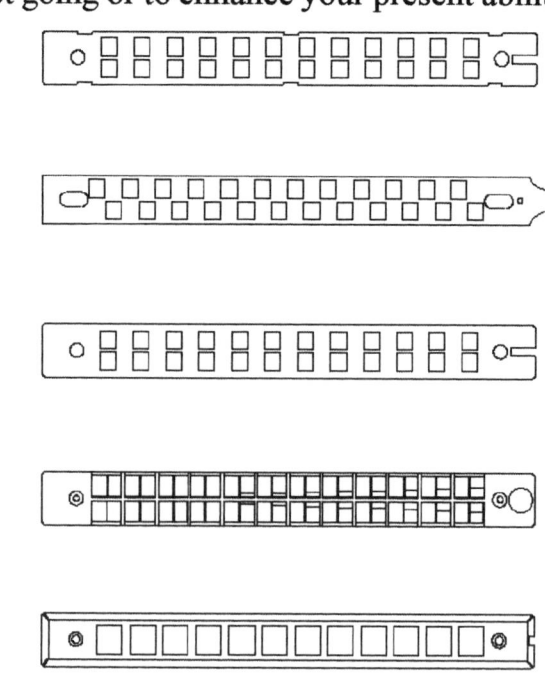

Play the Harmonica Well

PREAMBLE

I hope that your reason for playing the mouth organ is that you desperately want to make music and you love the sound it makes.

Any fool can make a noise on the harmonica, just pucker up and blow. Making music is different, and whichever style or type you choose it involves many, many subtle skills.

Think about a note. How loud is it? Does it change volume throughout its length? How does it change, loud to soft, soft to loud, swell in the middle? How does it start? Suddenly? Gradually? Has it got an accent? What tone is it being played with? Does this change? Has it got a vibrato? How does it end? Does it die away? Does it end abruptly? How does it relate to the previous note? How does it relate to the next note? How does it fit in with any other notes which are being played on the same or another instrument? And so on.

Take a phrase, or a section, or a whole piece of music, or a whole suite of pieces, or a complete concert, or series of concerts. All of these things take musical planning.

To make the planning and execution of your music as pain-free as possible you need an impeccable technique so that your chosen instrument does not get in the way of your musical expression.

The explanations, examples and mini musical exercises presented here will help you to go some way towards this goal.

OBSERVE!
When a note name is used in the text it will appear as follows:

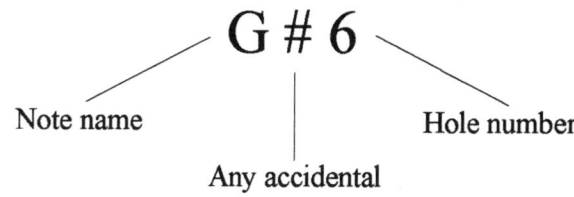

Note name — Any accidental — Hole number

Sometimes you will be asked to use B# instead of C and E# instead of F (i.e. alternative methods of producing the same note) A small circle is written above the note to be changed. It is used to help smoothness, breathing and make some chords possible. (I believe the notation of the circle was originated by Tommy Reilly.) When this is in written music it will be shown as:

means

Play the Harmonica Well

Holding

The harmonica is a slippery beast and needs firm handling to control it.

I will assume that you play the harmonica with the low notes to the left and the slide button to the right.. If you use the instrument the other way round just substitute 'right' for 'left' where needed.

Many people hold the instrument too close to the mouthpiece with the left-hand fingers. This at best means that mouth movement is restricted and at worst that you are wiping your nose the whole time. It is pretty obvious that the thumb and forefinger of the left hand are going to do most of the holding so get hold of the harmonica and then adjust your position as follows.

The cover-plates of the harmonica each have a ridge along the rear edge. Your left forefinger and thumb should be resting hard back against this ridge. While you are doing this look to see what is happening to the left hand end of the instrument. If your harmonica has 14 or 16 holes then your hand should be correct but with a 12 hole model do the following. Make certain that the BACK of the instrument is resting against flesh between thumb and forefinger (many people let the end of the harmonica rest here, this is not a good idea for your basic position).

Now that you have got the end correct look again at your finger and thumb. The first finger should be parallel with and resting against the ridge for as much of its length as possible. Don't let it angle in towards the mouthpiece. The thumb joint will be on the lower ridge slightly angled towards the mouthpiece.

Now lets do the right hand.

If the function of the left hand is to hold the instrument firmly then that of the right is to support the weight of the instrument, use the slider and provide the possibility of a vibrato. (See later) First put your forefinger on the button of the slide. To start with let the button rest in the crease of the first joint (from the nail end!). This may feel a little uncomfortable, but persevere, I'll explain a little later. The right hand back corner of the harmonica rests in the V between first and second fingers and your thumb should naturally be flat on the underside coverplate with the first joint on the ridge.

That's got both hands on the instrument, now to position them correctly relative to one another.

You may have curled the fingers of your right hand slightly round those of the left hand, fine, leave them like that. Now slide the left hand towards the right along the instrument until the heels of your hands are PRESSED together. The thumbs are lying next to each other, the left fitting against the right so that its nail ends just at the first joint of the right.

*P*lay the Harmonica *We*ll

You will most likely find that the fingers of your left hand are too long to fit comfortably with the right hand fingers, so let them curl a bit. Let the ends nestle in the lowest joint crease of the right hand fingers. If you have done this correctly you should have a nearly 'airtight' box made out of your hands. This is correct.

You may have noticed that having done all this the mouth-organ is at the wrong angle for your mouth! True, there is one more adjustment to make.

Do all of this next bit at once while keeping your hands together as arranged above. Swing the left elbow upwards until the forearm and mouth-organ are nearly horizontal. In doing this you will force the right forearm to become nearly vertical and the right hand to bend backwards at nearly a right angle. Now you can blow!. You will find this uncomfortable and awkward at first. Persevere, this position makes for great accuracy in your playing and gives a wonderful platform for producing a good tone. When everything becomes relaxed it is very easy to hold this position.

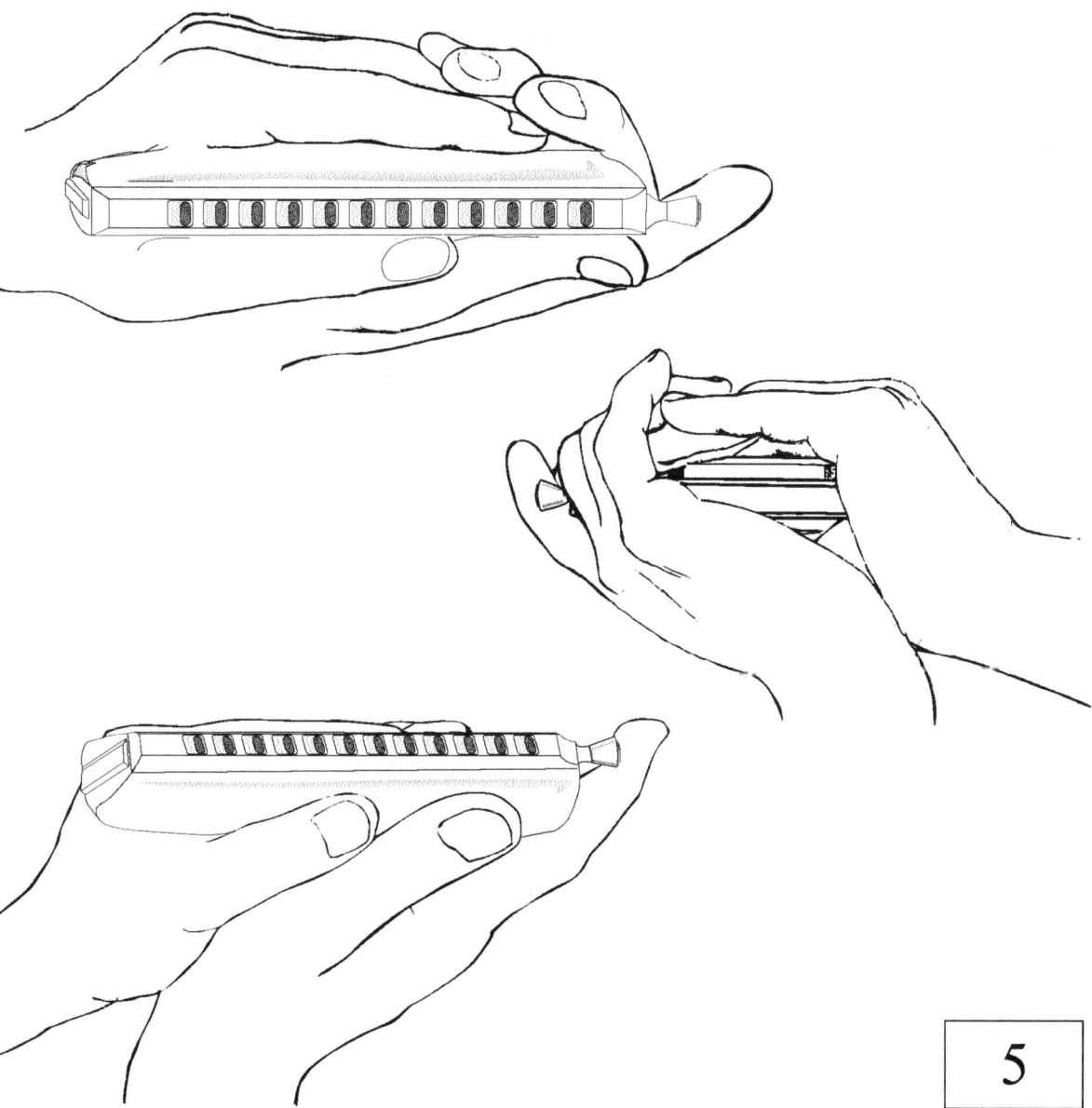

Play the Harmonica Well

POSTURE

Breathing is pleasant, it helps to keep you alive. It is also a major factor in your ability to play the harmonica. You cannot breathe correctly and efficiently unless your body is in a position to allow the ribcage and diaphragm free movement.

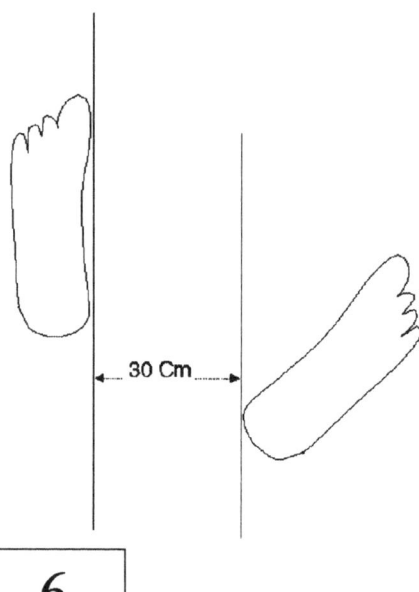

Sitting down to play

Try sitting down on a chair.

What happens to your body? All of a sudden you find there is a roll of fat at your waist, you have a curved spine and your abdomen is pressing up into your lungs stopping you breathing properly.

There is an easy way to sit down and breathe properly. To learn how to do this we have to get it right standing up!

Stand up straight and hold the harmonica as described in 'Holding'. How do you stand up straight? This will vary from person to person but try the following.

Feet about 30 Cm apart, left foot pointing straight forward, right foot further back (right toes on a level with the left foot heel) and angled slightly outwards. Rest your weight on the right foot. The point of your right elbow should end up vertically over the right toes. Lean very slightly backwards so that your spine feels a little curved and the abdomen muscles are taut. This should make you very upright. Breath in and out and you should feel the ability to take very deep breaths. You may have to move your right elbow very slightly outwards to give your rib cage room to move.

Try playing the instrument. Almost certainly you will find that your head has bent forward and at an angle to the right. By doing this you are restricting the airflow from your lungs. Try blowing into the instrument and straightening up your neck so that it is upright, and you are facing forward looking at a point about the same height as your head or slightly higher. As you do this you should notice a lessening of the restriction.

If you have adjusted yourself correctly you will almost certainly be feeling stiff and uncomfortable and think that this is an unnatural position. This is partly because you are unused to it and partly because we are not all built the same. Try to make yourself more comfortable without straying too far from the guidelines given.

Sitting down to play

Now for sitting down to play. It is useful to think of 'sitting down standing up' as this is the posture we are aiming at.

Only ever use a chair which is a comfortable height. The seat height should be such that the top of your legs are horizontal when your feet are flat on the ground. Don't worry about the chair back, you won't be touching it.

Stand about a foot length in front of the seat and marginally to the right of centre. You should be standing as described above. Now, leaving the left foot where it is, step back with the right and sit down on the front of the seat at the same time keeping the upper half of your body in precisely the same posture as for standing.

Play the Harmonica Well

As you sat down you would have felt uncomfortable about balance. This is due to the right leg. Put the right foot backwards just to the right of the front chair leg. The right knee drops when you do this and you will feel that you are being forced to sit upright.

This position is very comfortable and efficient. You should find that you can keep in this position without getting tired for a very long time.

Just for the fun of it, try bringing the right leg forward to rest next to the left and notice what happens to your spine and abdomen. Suddenly your breathing is restricted and there is that roll of fat again!.

Head, neck and collar

I have mentioned this elsewhere under a different heading and for a different reason. However, it bears repetition.

Whether you are sitting down or standing up your head should be in such a position that your eyes can look comfortably forward horizontally. If you get into this position you should find that breathing is easy and unrestricted. It is quite difficult to maintain this position as it is slightly unnatural.

When you can feel the position as being correct lower your chin and feel the restriction of your collar (if you have one) or just the neck flesh if you haven't.

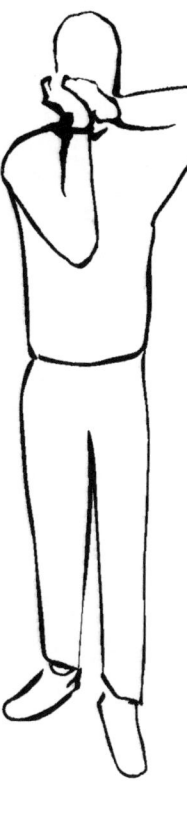

Play the Harmonica Well

MOUTH POSITION

This detailed explanation is long and complex. Try to follow the detail even if you can already use your tongue on the instrument. You may find that there is a slight alteration to your present position which could be beneficial

The position of your mouth and tongue on the mouthpiece and that of the tongue in your mouth while playing depends in detail on your physical make-up and has been shown but not explained in many harmonica books. The general principles are the same for most people. Basically you need to have your mouth over about 4 holes. Your tongue is used to block out the left-hand three leaving the right-hand one open and playable.

Notice that I say 'about' 4 holes. You will need to cover 5 holes exactly when you play octaves but for most of the time you could get away with less. The ideal is 4 holes and should be aimed at but some people will find the width physically tiring and this can get in the way of learning a good mouth position. If this is the case make the width about half a hole less (3 1/2) but not any smaller.

Stage 1

Sit down. (NOT as described in the section on posture but with knees together sitting relaxed and upright on a backed hard chair. This is just a preliminary exercise)

Lay your forefingers flat along the mouthpiece so that holes 3,4,5 and 6 are left open. The right hand forefinger covers holes 7,8,9 etc. and the tip of the finger just comes level with the left hand side of the bar between 6 and 7. The left forefinger is a mirror image of this (covering 1 & 2). Don't worry if the instrument feels a little insecure in your hands, it won't be like this for long! Put the instrument to your mouth so that the right hand corner of your lips just rests on top of the right forefinger nail. The left side of your mouth should be a mirror of this but don't worry too much if you fall a little short on this side. The instrument should not be tilted to favour either side of the mouth. Just for the moment keep your tongue off the mouthpiece. If you have done this correctly it will feel uncomfortable and not very far in your mouth! Now blow gently and you should hear four notes sounding, G3, C4, C5 and E6. The Cs will no doubt be rattling a bit as they are usually a little out of tune with each other.

Try taking the instrument out of your mouth and, still holding it as above, rest it on your knees. Yes! It is awkward. Wait a couple of seconds, relax, swing the instrument up slowly, and try blowing it again.

Note. You will be doing this sequence at every stage in this section as it makes your neck, arms and mouth relax between tries. This enables you to start each try from exactly the same position which speeds learning,

When you are confident that you are relaxed and can hear all four notes clearly go on to Stage Two. Do not rush this or any other stage, otherwise you are wasting both your time and money.

Stage Two

Everything the same as above .. except .. left forefinger off the mouthpiece. Use the left hand somehow to hold the instrument steady.

Play the Harmonica Well

Try to aim the mouth-organ into your mouth as before and blow. You should hear the four notes exactly as before but you are a little more comfortable and the sound should be a little better. If you cannot hear the four notes, try again. The trick is to get the left-hand side of the mouth to just replace the forefinger. Some people like to play the note and extract the left forefinger while it is sounding. Do whichever works for you.

It is important to master this stage. Do not even attempt the next stage until this one is really firm.

Stage Three

Start the same as Stage Two. When you are blowing gently feel along the mouthpiece with the tip of your tongue and listen to what happens to the notes. You should find that one or maybe two disappear in different places as you move it around.

This next bit is quite is difficult. Try always to aim the relaxed tip of your tongue at about the centre of hole 4 and gently positon it until the 'beating' of the two Cs ceases as your tongue stops up hole 4. Then the G3 and C5 should also go leaving the highest sounding note (E6). When you have a clear sound go to the next stage.

Note, many players have great difficulty at this point. Don't give up - it may take a few days for you to get it right.

Stage Four

Get a good clear E6 going as described above. Now ease the right hand finger out of the corner of your mouth. You should now have a good clean sound and it should, at last, feel fairly comfortable.

Stage Five

Now that you can blow a single note by this method try a draw note. Just play E6 as above. When you have a steady note change to draw. (F6). You may find that you get a little noise from D5 and/or A3. This is because it is natural to retract your tongue when breathing in. Try to compensate for this, it becomes natural very soon.

Stage Six

Become aware of the position of your lips on the cover-plates. You may find that the cover-plates are resting on the outside of the lips i.e. lips shaped as though you were about to say 'Pe' at the start of 'Pelican'. This can work but gives little flexibility. A good position which seems to give maximum flexibility to most players is as follows. Pout the lower lip outwards and rest the lower coverplate on the inside surface. This can seem fairly extreme at first but is very comfortable. The contact with the mouthpiece extends beyond halfway to the place where the inside of the lip joins the tooth roots!

Lastly, you must move onto a new note. This is covered in the next chapter.

Aim for clarity of sound. If you have not done this type of tongue blocking before you will notice that your tongue feels totally unmanageable and enormous! This feeling will disappear .... eventually.

I have resisted the temptation to draw a picture of what a cross section of the mouth playing a note looks like. If I did you would never believe it .... or try it!

Play the Harmonica Well

MOVEMENT

The cover-plates of a standard 12 hole chromatic are plated with nickel. This seems to have the property of sticking to your lips (even if damp!) and slipping in your hands (even when dry!).

After much use a patina of oxide, seen as a discoloration, will form on the surface and help a little. Some of the latest instruments appear to have stainless steel cover-plates which do not have this problem to the same extent.

The ideal instrument would move across the mouth with no resistance allowing a steady embouchure (mouth position) to be held. In practice there is always some dragging which can distort your mouth and make clear transition from one note to the next difficult. This dragging can be caused by lips sticking to the cover-plates and mouthpiece or the tongue being restrained by the edges of the holes. Although technique is important it also helps to have a good instrument with physical attributes which work with, rather than against, you!

A very good solution is to silver plate the cover-plates and mouthpiece. This is not expensive and well worth the effort. The feel is good, fingers stick to the surface and lips slide. Other materials have been tried (including wood!) but none seems as satisfactory as silver.

Some players have tried rounding off the corners of the mouthpiece holes to stop the sharpish edges catching on the tongue. If this is done very delicately it works. Too much rounding can leave you with no 'feel' for the position of the instrument and note-finding accuracy suffers. There are some Chinese instruments which have very comfortable round holes. They achieve this by having a countersunk entrance to the hole. It works well

There are a number of techniques for moving the instrument and a final method of playing will no doubt contain elements of most of them. However, it is easier to think about the various aspects separately.

Short Moves

First a movement from E6 to G7. Try to relax your mouth and tongue without allowing any laxness in the tone you produce. Fix in your mind what the two notes sound like either by experiment or thinking about it. Play the first note, think of the second note and when you are absolutely certain of where it is and what it will sound like .. move. To do the move just shift the left elbow, and thus the instrument, to the left. Mouth and tongue should not alter shape at all. Your head should remain stationary, just let the instrument slide.

Do this until you can move cleanly from one hole to another. Do not hurry, take three to four seconds to play the first note before moving like lightning to the second note. Even though the movement has to be fast there should be no jerkiness. The trick is to make the movement coincide with a slight change in breath pressure. (see below in the chapter on Breath Control)

Try to do the same thing first with F6 to A7 then E6 to A7, F6 to G7. When you have gained confidence with these do the same thing with the button pressed. (No, they do not feel the same!)

Slightly more difficult is the movement using the button on one of the notes but not on the other. Try E6 to G#7, then E#6 to G (more difficult) F#6 to G7, F6 to G#7. The actual technique is discussed in detail under 'Button movement' later on.

Play the Harmonica Well

In a nutshell .. the movement, change of breath and button press should occur at the same time, not in sequence.

I have just dealt with two holes here. It is up to you to work out similar routines on all the other holes. It is no good jumping about all over the place and having a go at every combination. Just do one or two each day for a couple of minutes. Do not hurry the process, spend as much time on the fourteenth try as you should have done on the first!

Longer Movements

This is really an extension of the above. The main problem is that you have to stop breathing as you pass over the unwanted holes. The faster you can make the move the easier it is to avoid unwanted notes sounding It becomes even more important to be certain what the note is that you are jumping to.

Maybe the greatest problem with the harmonica is that leaps are not constant. (G - D = a Fifth, so does B flat to F but one covers holes 3 - 5 and the other 3 - 6) and it is therefore quite hard for your body to learn the mechanical feel of a note the way you do on most instruments. Just imagine how it would be if a pianist suddenly had to reach an extra couple of Centimetres in the middle of a run of Fifths!

As the leaps get larger it becomes less practical to just move the instrument in a straight line. The reason for this is that you also have to move your arms and that is a lot of weight to move around. The obvious way to overcome this is to move the head to compensate. It is very difficult to stop yourself!

You must try, but the answer is a new technique.

Hold the instrument correctly but do not put it in your mouth. Try to imagine this next bit as though you were looking from above. Rotate the instrument so that the mouthpiece is first pointing to the right and then to the left. i.e. swing it through about a quarter circle. What should have happened is this. Your right forearm should have remained very nearly vertical and rotated. (the same sort of motion your wrist performs when unscrewing the lid of a stubborn jar) Your left wrist should have bent horizontally backwards and forwards. (the motion is the same as resting your forearm on a table and sweeping your fingers from right to left on the surface) While you are doing this rotation of the hands they must stay in the normal sound-box position. When you try this with the instrument in your mouth, the movement is very much more restricted, only a few degrees. This slight swing moves the instrument a surprisingly large distances across the mouth with little effort. However, it takes time to get it working. Up to Octave leaps using this method are fairly easy. For greater distances a combination of techniques is needed and slight head movement is almost inevitable.

Summing up.

The main aim is to keep your head and lips as still as possible and make the instrument do the moving.

Play the Harmonica Well

BREATH CONTROL

How to breathe

You already know how to stand, how to hold the instrument, how to put it in your mouth and shape your tongue. Now to put life into the mouth organ.

The standard joke aimed at harmonica players is .. 'How do you write your music then, blow, suck, suck, blow? ... Ha Ha Ha!' The trouble is that the thought of the word sometimes gets translated into action. The word 'suck' gives the impression of the action taken when drinking through a straw. The result of applying this to the mouth organ is a thin, nasty and non-controlled sound.

The title of this section is 'How to BREATHE' and this is just what you have to do. First of all find out how you breathe naturally, you may have to try a new method to get the best out of your instrument. This is not a definitive piece of medical research, but I notice three main types of breathing.

a   As you breathe in, the top of your chest, and possibly your shoulders, raise. They lower when you breathe out. There is little or no movement at 'belly' level due to the diaphragm and only a small volume of breath is used.

b   As you breathe in there is little or no movement at the top of your chest, shoulders remain stationary and your diaphragm extends to make you look a little 'potbellied'. Quite a large volume of air is used.

c   As you breathe in the top chest moves up followed by the diaphragm moving down. (you may do this in reverse, diaphragm first, top last) This is a combination of the other two without gross shoulder movement.

The last example is what you should aim at, breathing like a singer. There is one more dimension not covered so far, and that is the power use of the diaphragm.

I have mentioned already that the diaphragm is used to help breathing. It is also used to give controlled power to your notes. When you yawn you will find that there is a certain amount of tension in your diaphragm region. This is the type of feeling one should have most of the time while playing. This initial 'pressure allows you fine control of air pressure. It takes time for the muscles to develop, but that is true of most of the techniques in this book.

Breathing to start a piece

A piece of music does not just start. It needs to be prepared for. When you go to a concert there is a sense of excitement generated by the 'occasion'. This is enhanced by the preparation of the orchestra, the lights going down, the company etc. On a smaller scale each piece of music which you play should be prepared for before starting to play. Put it in a musical frame. How many times have you started a piece by hurriedly playing a test note and then launching straight in?

Play the Harmonica Well

Make sure that you are physically comfortable and ready to play. Everything is in the right place, music stand, music etc. Now comes the important bit. Think of the tune and its speed. Count to yourself a complete bar or couple of bars at this tempo. As you come towards the place in the bar where the tune starts, take as big a breath as necessary at the speed of the piece. This leaves you in a condition for a controlled start of the first note whether it is blow or draw.

Breathing to start a phrase

This is much the same as breathing to start the whole piece. If there is a substantial pause between phrases it is exactly the same technique. As the pause between the phrases gets smaller so the technique has to change. The time allowed for taking a breath becomes limited and you have to 'snatch' at air. This is where the technique of using the upper chest and the diaphragm comes into its own. It is possible to get a tremendous amount of air in a very short time. Try explosively breathing in using the diaphragm as the main muscle, near the end of the breath use the upper chest muscles. The diaphragm part is the same movement as the start of a fast yawn!

Breathing while playing a phrase

Sometimes you will find that you are running out of breath in the middle of a long passage. Running out can mean having too much air in you as well as being almost empty. Quite frequently this situation is just bad planning and a change in strategy can get you out of it on future occasions. However, there comes a time when you can see semiquavers stretching ahead to infinity. Something drastic has to be done if you are not to expire or blow up!

One ploy is to breath round the instrument whilst playing a note. This involves lifting, say, the top lip very slightly off the coverplate and allowing air to escape either in or out. You can also allow air to escape through your nose. Fairly naturally it is 'in' on a draw note and 'out' on a blow note! The trick is to do this without allowing the tone colour of the note to alter. This, as with many things in this book, takes time and effort to get it right.

If none of the above gives you relief you may sometimes be able to miss a nonessential note and take a quick sip. (Flute transcriptions of Bach are full of notes marked for 'miss and breath if you have to'.) If you try this do make certain that the note really is nonessentials.

One final method is a technique used by recorder players and some reed players .. circular breathing. (OK, so you have heard of a flautist who uses it as well) This involves using your tongue as a piston on the air in your mouth to keep the flow going while you breath in (or out) through your nose. To date this seems to have been little used and a very limited technique for the harmonica player. However it has been useful to me on a few occasions. I feel that it is an area well worth exploring.

Sometimes you may find that it is musically inappropriate to breath at the start of a phrase.

If this is the case .. don't!

There is a technique covered in the chapter on articulation which helps to start the phrase cleanly.

Play the Harmonica Well

Articulation

Notes do not just happen, they have to be carefully crafted.

The previous sections have explained the gross movement of air, here we deal with its fine control in starting and stopping. This is possibly the most important aspect of playing the harmonica and is the equivalent of bow technique on a violin or tonguing on a wind instrument. There are several ways to start your breath moving. You already have years of experience of normal breathing, that is one! You can use your tongue (as though you were saying 'Tu', 'Tut' or 'Tuk'. Some people find that this works well for them, but it tends to give a rather thin sound. The method I am going to concentrate on is the use of the 'throat'.

For the Classical Harmonica player (and perhaps for all harmonica players) the use of the 'throat muscles' is fundamental to a wide-ranging technique.

A word about the 'muscles' used. Whereas the throat is mentioned it means the vocal chords and the use of the glottal stop. If this sounds technical then a simple explanation follows.

When you cough there is a buildup of pressure in your lungs - the pressure is contained by closing your vocal chords. The actual cough is caused by relaxing the vocal chords and allowing the sudden explosive release of the pressure. The noise of the cough is partly friction of the air passing over various bits of the mouth and partly the vocal chords vibrating. (A lot of coughing is to dislodge mucus or food from the vocal chord area and the vibration of the air can help this)

A short cough is made by relaxing and closing the vocal chords fairly rapidly. In a modified form this is all that "throat control", "throat vibrato", "staccato control" etc. consists of. That last sentence is rather like saying "the Mona Lisa is only a bit of paint put on canvas". To make the "cough" into a useful tool needs practice and rigid self-appraisal.

Long notes started with the throat

Play a note by breathing it. You will hear that the note starts softly and gets quickly louder until it reaches it's full volume. It will stay at this volume level until you stop the breath. This is a slack method of playing a note and gives minimal control. (It is a valuable additional method of playing a note but should not be first choice) The envelope of sound most likely is like this:

Now try this:
Cough gently into the instrument. Make as little 'cough' noise as possible. You will notice that the note starts more cleanly (although its continuation is most likely very erratic!) More about this later.

Play the Harmonica Well

Try playing the same note three or four times one after the other (about two per second). Do not try to produce a string of 4,000 notes stretching into tomorrow at this stage. Keep it to small groups with a few seconds rest, thought and analysis in between. The aim is to keep the muscle from getting tired. The vocal chords are tremendously strong and supple but the strength and control we need to use are different to their normal usage. This control must be built up slowly if it is to be effective and long lasting.

The notes you are producing will most likely die away rapidly after the nice clean start. (like this)

Now you have to make them stay at the same volume level over the complete length of the note. Like this:

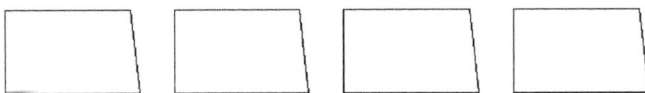

Here is a 4 stage plan to make the notes better:

Without the mouth-organ in your mouth say 'Aaaaah' - making it last a couple of seconds.

Do the same thing again, but this time don't make any sound with your vocal chords except for the initial click. It should sound as though you are leaking! There is a point to watch here. Some people find that they are imitating a sigh. This is not correct as there is not the same control needed for a sigh. Make the whole thing a definite 'word'. Notice how you are controlling the way the air goes out of your lungs by the lower ribs and the diaphragm.

Try the light cough you are now so good at to start the word Aaaaah. Keep the diaphragm constant throughout the word. This should feel really positive but not strained.

Now try stage three with the harmonica in your mouth. You should produce a brilliant note - constant in volume and with a clean start. This is a fundamental technique. It is easy(ish) on a blow note and not nearly so easy on a draw note.

Phrasing

This has two aspects, the artistic and the purely technical.

Phrasing a set of notes is the effort made by the player to give that group special qualities. Each 'phrase' should have meaning as a group and sound as though the notes flow together. The group should fit in with those around it and have meaning within the overall plan of the piece.

When music is phrased properly the listener should be aware of the ebb and flow of interest, intensity, volume as we are all aware of the same characteristics within a spoken sentence. In speech these attributes are subtle and the same should apply to musical phrasing.

How does a phrase work? In a way it is just a mini tune, it has a start, a journey and an end. In a beautifully turned phrase the whole journey should feel as though it is aiming towards the end with nothing to interrupt it. As such you must use the normal technical tools for starting a note to also start a complete phrase.

Earlier I have mentioned the throat for starting a note, use it here. Decide how the phrase should start. Should it be gentle, hard, loud, soft, percussive or delicate? The throat control you have learnt will enable you to do all of these things.

Decide how the phrase should be shaped. Where is its high point, the place of maximum intensity before it comes to its end (if it does not end on a climatic note)? Is there more than one 'high' point in the phrase, if so which one is the major? Is the lead up to the climax sudden or gradual, does it have several steps in volume or a 'shaped' volume envelope? Should you change tone as you go through the phrase or aim to keep it the same and change it on the next phrase?

Decide how to end your phrase. Does it fade out or end suddenly? Is there a silence between this phrase and the next or does it want to almost join and flow into the next?

If your phrase is to be smooth then you have several problems. The main one is how to disguise the tremendous difficulties of changing from blow to draw, draw to blow, using the button and leaping from one hole to another (and combinations!). This is dealt with elsewhere.

When you have sorted out this 'disguise' problem the next hurdle is controlling changes in volume and/or tone over several notes. It is easy to make a single note increase or decrease in loudness, but much practice and hard listening is needed to get a true increase in the start of the next note. The main danger is that the volume goes up in steps where the step is the start of the next note. To get over this try playing a number of alternating notes at a constant volume note to note. Endeavour to make a stream of notes with no obvious 'bumps' in it When you can achieve this, then and only then, try increasing or decreasing volume. A fair analogy is walking on thin ice! Every step must be catlike and smooth, otherwise .. crunch .. you are cold and wet.

Play the Harmonica Well

Master of disguise!

A great deal of the technique of playing the harmonica is that of disguising the fact that you cannot play a true legato on the thing. This is because of the unique feature that we blow and draw rather than blow steadily. To get over this we have to fool the listener into thinking that a legato is being heard when it is not!

First point. It is easy to get a legato between A3 and B4. Just slide the instrument and keep on drawing!. It is very difficult to get a legato between F2 and G3, change of breath, change of hole. Solution? Simply make all the note changes as crummy as the worst one! I am NOT advocating sloppy playing, far from it. You must make your most difficult movements and breath changes as perfect as possible. When you have achieved a very good standard on these difficult note changes make all the other changes in the scale sound exactly the same, warts and all. Because all the changes now sound the same you will be giving a much better impression of a legato than by having some of them perfect and some flawed.

Second point. If you find it difficult to do a large leap smoothly, make the second note a little softer than the first. The 'hanging' sound from the first note will disguise the gap before the second note and the lesser attack on the second will not emphasise your shortcomings! There is another technique using both sides of the mouth for long leaps, this is explained later under 'Tongue Switching'.

Third point. In some Baroque pieces there is a sequence of notes where a melody note low down is alternated with one or more accompaniment notes. The melody must be brought out and the accompanying notes given less importance. The trick here is to hold the melody note on firmly for as long as possible and then play the lesser notes a little less firmly and a trifle softer. Almost overdo the time length of the melody note.

Fourth point. Making the note sound after you have stopped playing. The impression is that the note is still tailing off into silence after you have actually finished blowing. This is a way of ending phrases before a rest or at the end of a piece where the impression must be of calm peacefulness. To get the right effect you must die away the breath as normal but as it dies take the harmonica a little way out of your mouth so that the air escapes round the instrument. This helps the smooth decrescendo. The effect is heightened for an audience if the instrument is kept in position for quite a long time after the note has actually died. If you are really engrossed in the music you will find that this happens naturally, but it is a good conscious ploy when you are a little uncertain!

SUSTAIN

Play the Harmonica Well

TONE MANIPULATION

"Tone must be appropriate to the style of music being played, position in the music and relative to tones around it."

The beauty of the harmonica is that it has such a wide range of tone. I think it is possible to say without too much exaggeration that the harmonica has the widest tonal (and stylistic) range of any instrument. This can, however, lead to all sorts of excesses when playing.

What is Tone? The purest sound is a note which contains no 'overtones' or 'harmonics' just the basic note. Not only is it boring but it has no character. There is no natural instrument which can play this sort of sound although it can be achieved on electronic instruments. When a string is vibrated we can see it forming a sort of loop, like a skipping rope. If the string is touched in the centre as it vibrates it forms two loops and sounds an octave higher. If the string is touched at a Third or Quarter of the way along three and four loops are formed and the notes sound a Fifth and a Fourth above.

Does all this have any bearing on our sound? Yes, because all instruments produce a mix of these 'harmonics'. It is this mix which allows us to identify an individual type of instrument and even a particular one. The number and intensity of harmonics for a particular note on a particular instrument is its fingerprint and the way we recognise it.

Most instruments are well behaved and produce harmonics as described above. Not the harmonica! Our instrument (and all free reed instruments) produce really weird harmonics with funny numbers as multiples. This is why we have such an astounding range of sounds available. The basic mish-mash of unusual harmonics gives the harmonica richness. We manipulate this with hands, mouth etc., to produce the particular sound we want.

Tone must be appropriate to the style of music being played, position in the music and relative to tones around it. For example, it would be inappropriate to play the Malcolm Arnold harmonica concerto using the sounds and tones created by blues players. It would be equally silly to play blues with a classical tonal outlook.

There is a school of thought which says 'purest is best'. A sweet and lovely tone throughout a piece can be utterly boring. Listen to any great player on any instrument and you will hear subtle (and gross) variation even within a single note to make a musical statement. The whole point is that, however extreme or different, it must be appropriate to the stylistic needs of the music and the intentions of the composer. This skill can only be learned by playing masses of music of all sorts, and by listening to music of all styles by great players of all instruments. Listen to Heifitz and Grappelli (violin), Rubenstein and Oscar Petersen (piano) Honneger (oboe), Du Pres (cello), Rampal (flute), Beckett and Armstrong (trumpet), Artie Shaw and Jack Brymer (clarinet), Glennie and Fry (percussion), Bream and Reinhardt (Guitar) and about 50,000 others! Oh yes! How about Adler and Theilemans (harmonica)?

It is impossible to cover the whole subject effectively in

Play the Harmonica Well

print in a reasonable number of pages. But, let us look at a simple example to illustrate the problem.

Play 8 quavers all on E6. There are many things which can be done to these notes. Play smoothly with little gap. Staccato (semi-quaver, semi-quaver rest). Gradual change from smooth to staccato. Speed up. Slow down. Crescendo. Decrescendo. Swell towards the middle. Combinations of some of these. Try them all.

If you had these eight notes in a piece you would have to decide if any one of the combinations was appropriate. However, this is not what this section is about. In addition to the above it is also possible to alter the tone in many subtle ways. Closed to open hands or the reverse. Change throat shape or mouth shape. Combine the two. Go from a sharp sound to a full smooth sound etc. These can also be used in combination with the other variations mentioned above. The combinational possibilities are endless!

It is obvious that this section is advice, not tuition! The final bit of advice is .... listen, listen, listen, and analyse what you hear. Then go away and experiment, and really listen to yourself, not on a tape recorder but as you play (but see below). Be very self-critical. Know when to reject an idea and when to pursue it. When you are firmly convinced that you have got it right, leave it for a few days, or weeks, and then try again. It is amazing how your feelings will have changed.

In a nutshell .. listen, try, keep an open mind and keen ears.

Note. As always, a dogmatic statement can come back and haunt you!. Recently I have heard a DAT tape recorder. It was the size of a pack of cigarettes (remember them?). The sound from this amazing little Sony recorder was better than a lot of studio equipment I have worked with. In my opinion you would get a very good idea of what you sounded like from this type of machine. However, this little box cost over £500 and the tapes about £15 each at the time of writing.

Use of mouth, throat and diaphragm

The use of the air path for breathing is dealt with elsewhere, here we are only concerned with the air path as a manipulator of tone.

Speaking is a task which occupies a lot of our waking hours. It is the most difficult exercise we undertake in our whole lives and involves many complex and subtle actions. We can harness some of these actions to enhance the quality and variety of the tone we give to the harmonica sound.

When we speak we create a certain voice tone. Depending on our physical make-up, nervous tension, subject, education and upbringing so our voices may be plummy, squeaky, thin, rich etc.. Most people can put on a 'posh accent' or imitate a particular type of voice with a little

*"The final bit of advice is .... **listen, listen, listen,** and analyse what you hear. Then go away and experiment."*

Play the Harmonica Well

bit of effort, even though it is outside our normal characteristics. We do this by listening and adjusting the vocal path, air pressure, position of tongue and lips etc. These same techniques are used to alter the tone of the harmonica.

Again this section is more advice than detail. Try altering your mouth shape whilst playing a note. Change the basic shape from AAAAH to EEEEE, from OH to OOOOH. Try opening your throat and tensing your diaphragm. How? Easy, pretend you are yawning and then play! I find that this one technique gives me more tonal power than any other 'internal' trick.

Some people can use their sinus regions to enhance the tonal characteristics. I'm afraid that I was created with blocked sinuses and when they occasionally clear I can't play. For this reason I cannot give advice on this technique. However, be aware that it is a possibility.

Use of hands - or how to play loud softly!

Hands can be a help or hindrance in tone production. The indiscriminate use of flapping digits and palms can make a musical mockery of an otherwise well played piece. Yes, this is a matter of opinion, but you would be wise to think about it!

I will deal with the vibrato side of tone production later, for the moment lets look at nearly static hands and see what they contribute to the overall sound coming from the instrument.

When you blow across the neck of a bottle you get a fixed pitch sound. When you shout near a brick wall you hear an echo coming back. Your hands can be used to emulate both of these effects on the harmonica.

First the important 'bottle' technique. This works because the bottle contains a certain volume of air which you can set vibrating with your breath. The pitch is 'fixed' in that it always sounds the same note. Put a bit of water in and the pitch goes up. With some bottles you can also overblow and produce a fixed higher sound. A similar thing happens when you cup your hands round the mouth organ and play a note. If you adjust your hand position carefully it is possible to get the same resonating effect. The first time you try this it is remarkably difficult and you will only be able to make it work on one or two notes. Gradually, as you become aware of the sounds you are creating the range will become bigger.

This technique enables you to play very loudly, with good tone, with very little physical effort and does not strain the harmonica reeds (so the instrument will last longer).

Hold the instrument as described in the 'Holding' section above. Play G7 at about middle to low volume. While you play, adjust the volume of your hand space very, very gradually. Listen carefully to the sound you produce. The hand movements to find the sound should be very small and gradual. It is no good flapping around like a demented butterfly. Move in steps of a millimetre if you

This is one area where it is a good idea to get hold of a teacher to listen to you and advise.
The odd few pounds you spend on the session will be repaid a thousand times by the ease with which you can build a big sound.

Play the Harmonica Well

can. As you approach the correct position you will find that the tone and intensity of the note alters radically. You will then be able to 'go out the other side' by continued movement. It is best to try this exercise in a fairly resonant room to start off with as it will help.

When you first get this sound it may be weak and not much above the level of your ordinary playing for that breath pressure. If you work on it you will find that it will gradually get more intense and full. This will be the result of your brain doing subtle adjustments to your hand, mouth and breath which comes about through listening carefully to what is happening. You should get the impression of filling your head with sound. The effort to produce it should be negligible.

This is the technique which has enabled me to play with orchestras without amplification and still have my harmonica in tune after 30 plus years.

When you have the effect firmly on G7 try to extend the range, SLOWLY, one note at a time. Try A7 and when this is firm, B7. You will notice that as you go higher the hollow in your hands has to get bigger. This seems to be out of step with the law which seems to say 'bigger = lower'. However, that is the way it appears to happen. This effect works well in the mid part of the instrument but becomes increasingly difficult as you approach the extremes of range.

Here is a technique which is of no use whatsoever! You will never use it but it will give you an idea of how the hands actually work.

Play a note, say G7, holding with the left hand only. With your right hand formed into a nearly flat palm with the fingers together wave it in front of the harmonica between 1 and 3 feet away from it, palm facing the back of the instrument. I do this by dropping the hand to about waist level and flapping it up and down (about 2 seconds to a flap!!) towards the back of the instrument. Listen to what happens to the sound you are making. Do it very slowly and you will find that the distance of your hand from the mouth organ affects the quality of sound, even a couple of feet away. Having said that this technique is useless, I have seen a busker in the London Underground using it to good financial effect!

If you can master the technique of 'playing loudly softly' then you have a very valuable tool.
You will save a considerable amount of money on instruments.
You will be able to hold your own with other instruments.
You will have a vastly increased range of sound.
You will have more physical energy to spare for the other aspects of playing.

Vibrato

A word about what a vibrato really is. One thing is certain, most mouth organ players do not use it! On all 'conventional' instruments a vibrato is produced by raising and lowering the PITCH of a note by a small amount several times a second. (Think of the movement a cellist makes, rolling the left-hand finger up and down the neck, shortening and lengthening the string.) Larry Adler is one of the few players who approaches this ideal with his lip and tongue vibrato, but this puts tremendous pressure on the reeds and quickly puts them out of tune. On a wind instrument the same effect is obtained by tensing the lip and similar techniques. What we tend to do on the harmonica is alter the VOLUME and TONAL CONTENT of the note, not the pitch. Having said that, we do make quite a nice job of it! The two different types of vibrato described here are both of the 'harmonica type'.

Hand Vibrato

There are many different ways in which the hands can make a vibrato.

Flapping the left hand fingers while keeping the right hand still can be effective but is very difficult to control. This method has the advantage that it leaves the right hand to deal with support and button operation. Flapping the right hand fingers is usually easier for a right handed person but the results are equally unpredictable. The effectiveness and musicality of these two methods depends on the player.

In my opinion, the best way to approach the whole problem is to look for a method which demands the least physical movement for maximum effect with easiest control and smallest effort.

Above you will find a section describing the production of a big sound by using the hand cavity. It is possible to use this effect to obtain a very efficient hand vibrato. This is difficult to describe because of the very small movements involved, be careful how you interpret the words.

Hold the instrument correctly and get a good fat sound using the 'playing loud softly' method, use G7 to start with. The vibrato consists of moving in and out of the resonance point. To do this the right wrist rotates very slightly in and out. Here are three ways of visualising it.

a The effect is of pushing the right wrist outwards away from you and bringing it back ... about 2 - 4 mm!
b If the heels of your hands are correctly positioned together you could think of it as rubbing the base of the right thumb across the base of the left thumb.
c If the fingers of the right hand are slightly curled round those of the left it is like rocking the right hand on the left hand forefinger where it touches the right hand forefinger. (thus alternately pressing the little and first fingers of the right hand against those of the left)

In each case the change in sound is the thing to concentrate on. Only do enough movement to make it happen. The better your 'resonance' effect, the less the

Play the Harmonica Well

movement you need. On very good notes at very loud volumes you may sometimes get away with movements as small as a millimetre. When you first start this it will feel awkward and stiff, persevere, it will soon loosen up and become very natural (where have I said that before??). The higher you go up the instrument, the larger becomes the hand movement until you may be using almost 2 Cm very high up.

Throat Vibrato

There appears to be a variety of ways to produce the sound harmonica players generally recognise as being a 'throat vibrato'. Most are controlled by muscles in the upper region of the respiratory system. There is, however, a method used naturally (and very effectively) by some players using the diaphragm muscles to control alternating pressure. This is difficult and I do not know of an effective way of teaching it.

Until a few years ago most players experimented for years to get a throat vibrato because of the richness of the sound which one or two professionals were obtaining. This trial and error approach has resulted in some marvellous variations and a great deal of frustration! The method of learning the technique described here is both easy to do and a part of what I hope is an already established practice within your playing.

Look again at the section on how to use the glottal stop to do staccato notes and start phrases. Make certain that you can do a series of slow staccato notes on, say, G3. Do about four per second.

When you have established your ability to do this comfortably try the following. Make each note rapidly die away by only giving the reed the initial 'kick'. When this is happening you should find that if you relax the 'cough' just a little the sounds will begin to join up. Keep the control on diaphragm pressure which you need for staccato notes. If you look at the diagrams it may help you visualize the steps towards the vibrato.

When you first start this you may find that the speed runs away from you and you end with a series of rapid-fire grunts! This is not right!! You must keep the repetition rate exactly steady. Keep starting from a few staccato notes and softening into the vibrato, this way you will establish the good habit quickly. You will find that this works well over the range C1 to about C5 but is much more difficult above these notes.

I have dealt with blow notes. Draw notes are easier to tackle once you can actually produce an embryonic throat vibrato. It is more difficult for most players to make staccato draw notes and in the early stages this also applies to the vibrato.

It is possible to make the sound of a drowning animal gasping its last when trying this technique, please aim for beauty!

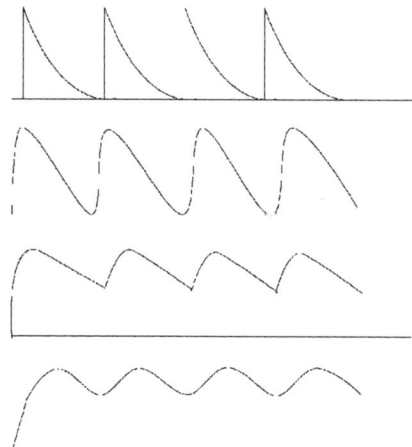

Tone usage

A brief note about 'tones' and effects in general. Just because you can do a particular thing does not mean that you must or that it will be appropriate. I well remember playing for the first time with a professional string quartet, also for the first time live on Radio 3. After we had been rehearsing for a little while the leader took me on one side and said ' In this music we are trying to depict a beautiful love affair, please do not turn it into a rape with bells and whistles'. Looking back I am very grateful to him. There is a lovely picture by Paul Klee of fishes. In it is one tiny spot of brilliant red. That one discrete spot makes the whole picture. The same is true of musical effects, appropriate, least and discrete is usually best.

Button movement

The slide movement on harmonicas has a lot to answer for! There are two main designs, the old traditional type with a short slide action and the newer model with twice the length of travel. It would be nice to say that they both had advantages but this is not true for the advanced player.

The traditional slider

This is usually made up of three pieces: a slider, flat base piece and a channelled top piece. The slide has small staggered holes and the other two pieces have 'in-line' holes. There are some disadvantages to this design the main one being that it is punched out of thin metal. Because of poor manufacture these pieces are always bowed across their width leading to quite large air leaks. This can be overcome with a little gentle 'engineering' by the player resulting in a wonderful increase in volume and tone control. The central slider is a little flimsy and bends easily meaning that sometimes the slide binds and is difficult to move smoothly.

The size of the holes is about right to give a little resistance to air flow which helps control but means that you have to work at getting a big sound.

The new slider

This comprises the slider, a flat bottom piece and a channel cut in a shaped mouthpiece. The holes in the slider are still staggered but they are twice as long. The reasoning behind this is, apparently, because beginners have trouble with some notes due to poor control of airflow. This might be a fair argument for a beginners instrument, but to extend the idea to the professional instrument costing many hundreds of pounds is ludicrous. Imagine telling a top line violinist that they had to use thick strings because beginners found them easier!

The longer movement of the slide detracts from the degree of control obtainable with the traditional one. It is not possible to use as fast for turns and trills.

Mechanically there appear to be problems with cutting the channel in the mouthpiece. This results in unpredictable loss of air in certain areas of an instrument which are

Play the Harmonica Well

VERY hard to cure. The latest instruments have a further problem in that the cover plates can push the whole slide assembly slightly off the body.

Normal slide changes

The positioning of the forefinger on the button has already been discussed (Holding).

The most frequent slide use is a change from one note to another which is sharpened. It may sound simplistic to say 'Just push the slide in with your forefinger', but I wonder if this is what you actually do? I believe you will find that your other fingers on the right hand move in sympathy. You most likely contract your whole hand slightly as well! Try to minimise the involvement of any other part of your hand so that the desired speed and agility can be concentrated where it is needed. Have you thought that going from, say, C# to C is just as difficult as going from C to C#. Some would say more difficult because it is hard to be positive about letting go of something. You will need to practice this.

The main practical difficulty is not always the button but the combination of button, breath and possibly movement at the same time. Getting this right on one note may be easy, but getting it so that it sounds the same on all combinations of breathing and hole movement will tax you to the limit.

Now to practicalities

Here is a very difficult task for you. Play C#.

Did you manage it? I wonder? Here is what may have happened. You put the instrument in your mouth, adjusted the position, pressed the button and blew. In that order. That is not playing the note C#, that is doing a series of actions What should be happening is this. The mouth organ should arrive in position, the button should be pressed and breath started at exactly the same time. Here is a little exercise which should help you to get it right. Play the scale of C# starting hole 5. (C# D# E# F# G# A# B# C#) Easy.

Now play it by starting each note in the scale as described above and finishing it by stopping breath, and letting out the button at the same time. This scale will sound very chopped up. You should only hear the notes listed and no slurs into or out of the note. Try this slowly and work up the speed. An eventual metronome = 108 with two notes to the beat is about right. When you have achieved this comfortably make the notes sound as long as possible, keeping to the same speed. Make the gap between the notes as short as possible.

This is a frustrating exercise, you will find that some notes are harder to get right than others. Think about it. This is exactly the same problem as moving about the instrument in general. There is however the added problem of using the button at the same time.

Play the Harmonica Well

TRILLS AND TURNS

It is very easy to press the button a number of times very quickly. This is not necessarily a trill! It usually is an unmusical sound which makes musicians cringe.

The harmonica is very good at doing some semi-tone trills (C-C#, F-F# etc.), less good at others (F#-G, C#-D etc.). It is quite good at some whole tone trills (A-B, B flat - C etc.), atrocious at most others (B-C# etc.). (There is a new technique emerging using tone bending which may help. This is not well enough established to see whether or not it is a way forward yet and so is not described here).

Unless otherwise specified by the composer or by ethnic tradition all trills use the notes of the scale you are playing in. If this happens to be a Major key then the only two semi-tone trills are between 3rd - 4th and between 7th and Octave. Even these cannot always be played well (F#-G in the G scale).

The best advice to do with trills is .. DON'T !! Only use a trill if it is musically correct and well within your technique.

Remember that a trill should be from one note to the next in the scale you are playing in at the time. i.e. if you are in key C then a trill on G would be G A G A, if you were in Ab it would be G Ab G Ab

One of the main problems with doing a trill of any kind is that it is made easier if you shift your hands into a different position. The trouble with this is that the tone alters radically when you do it! The trill MUST fit in with the tone and volume pattern of the phrase it is in. There are two ways of achieving this. The first is to make sure that you are playing with the same tone before you come to the trill. Surely not the best solution. The trill should not dictate the tone colour of the rest of the music. The second way is difficult but better. Make certain that the rest of your hand position is not affected by rapid use of the button. This takes a lot of work .. maybe months. No! ... *Certainly* months!

Another problem arises from the fact that the word 'trill' has meant 'fast button movement' to most of us harmonica players since we started playing. 'Good, here is a nice long trill, twiddle, twiddle for a second or two and think of something else." Not So! A trill is really just a short section of fastish notes with a repeat pattern and sometimes a tail at the end to lead into the next note. The difficulty arises from trying to perform them musically. The only way to get around this is to work at trills in all positions with all sorts of turns at the end. Add them to your repertoire only when you can do them neatly. In other words take a leaf out of every other instrumentalists' method book.

Part button movement

You may have noticed that using the slider on the harmonica tends to cut up a line of notes. There is a minute gap between the pressed and non pressed sound. This is partly because you are playing correctly!

Play the Harmonica Well

There are times when it is possible, and desirable, to get rid of this gap and smooth out the transition. The obvious reason for using the technique is to make a mordent smoother, for example A-B flat-A. If you play an A and then slowly press the slider you will hear the A and Bflat sound together and then the A stop. The A stops well before the button is fully home. Now play the A again but this time tap the button just hard enough to make the Bflat sound, but not enough to make it go right home, and then let go. Do this delicately but fast and you should find that you have an elegant sounding triplet.

You would be right in thinking that this seems a lot of work for such a limited technique. You will find that there are one or two other places where you use it, turning the corner at the top of some scale passages for example. It also pays off in giving more awareness of what is actually happening when using the button and considerably more control.

Definitions

There follow a few definitions of the more common turns and trills. This will get you going. For an in-depth treatment of the subject try one or more of these books:
Ornaments and Abbreviations for Examination Candidates by William Lovelock, published by William Elkin Music Services.
A handbook of Musical Knowledge, James Murray Brown, published Trinity College.

I do not recommend the theory books by Associated Board, the are muddling.

Acciaccatura (pronounced atch-a-ca-too-ra)

Play the little grace note on the beat as lightly and swiftly as possible. Notice the line through the small note.

Appoggiatura (pronounced ap-poj-a-too-ra)

Notice that there is no line through the small note.

Mordent

Do the twiddle at the start as quickly and gracefully as you can, do not make it sound hurried.

Inverted Mordent

Same as for the Mordent above

Play the Harmonica Well

Ornamentation can be a life study. There is so much to learn. The basics of ornamentation are easy and mostly the common sense interpretation of sensible and practical signs written by one workman for another.

Turn (Also called Gruppetto)

Turns are an art form all of their own. The arrangement of notes varies depending on whether the sign is above the note or after it. This is where a specialist book is needed. Below is another example and here the notes are altered from the scale by the signs on the ornament.

Trill

In modern music any fancy twists and turns around a trill are usually written out for you by the composer. In ancient times you were supposed to know your trade and be aware of what all the esoteric signs meant.

One problem which emerged was that different composers meant different things by the same or similar signs. Also there were sometimes regional and national differences. This further complicates the issue and makes the authentically correct interpretation of signs on music quite a challenging pastime. Take heart, start simple and add as you learn.

In the violin repertoire (and for most other classical instruments) there are many books of studies and exercises devoted to the art of trill and turn. Most of these are totally inappropriate for the harmonica but it is worth while looking through Scale and Study books to see if there is any thing which might help you. At the end of this book is a selection of the books and pieces I have found helpful both for technical exercises and furthering knowledge.

Projection

There is an old joke about the sound of the bagpipe .. the further away it is, the finer it sounds! In some ways the same can be said for the harmonica sound. Let me explain.

The closer you are to the back of the harmonica the more you will hear breath and throat, clothing rustle, slide clicks etc. amongst the musical sounds. You will also hear the difference in position of the notes at the top of the instrument and those at the bottom. The position of the hands will make a drastic change to what you hear as well. If you change the position of your head, either distance or angle, the sound will appear to change again.

As the listener gets further away from the instrument the mechanical noises die away but the musical sounds mellow and form a more solid soundscape. Another factor is that the reflections from the room (echo) start to have an effect on the overall sound. It is possible to use this to enhance your volume and tone by experimenting with your position in a room or hall. Aiming your sound at different parts of the room has a big effect. It takes some experience, and the help of friends, to know just what the effects are. However you will usually find that the position which makes *you* feel happiest is the right one.

A problem for the harmonica player who does recording for television or radio is that the sound engineers always prefer to 'mike' very close, usually within a few inches. This is done to isolate the sound from other instruments. This can give the worst of all possible worlds. You have to rely on the engineer for the final sound, so make certain that you discuss it with him. The best microphone position for me seems to be just above and in front of my left hand. However this is a very personal matter of taste. If the studio demands that you play in a solo booth then you must use headphones to get feed back of what everyone else is playing. You also need feedback of what *you* are playing. Getting the right balance between these two demands can take a little time. Do not be afraid to make your desires known. You have seen the mistakes even the best of stars make in the annual 'Aunties Bloomers' type of program. Everyone makes mistakes and everyone needs time to get comfortable.

It is far more difficult to project into a 'dead' room than a 'live' one. Lots of drapes make the room feel very hard work. For the listener this usually means that they can hear the real sound of your instrument. This is not always what you want!

Some players do all their practise in a lively room such as a bathroom or kitchen. This is great for the ego but not too good for the development of the strongest and biggest sound.

Finally, if you are playing to an audience, do just that. Make certain that they can see that you are playing to each and every one of them. At some time you should have looked at everyone of the audience!

Play the Harmonica Well

WHICH HOLE?

It may seem perfectly obvious which hole to use for a particular note on the harmonica. After all, there is only one G at the hole 3 level and if we want that note, that's the one we've got to play.
True?

Because of the peculiar physical makeup of the harmonica and the fact that there are only seven different notes in a major scale we have a problem. If we are to have two notes in one hole (blow and draw) this gives (C D), (E F), (G A), (BC). The logical sequence would have been blow, draw in each hole. This would have left B as Blow and C as Draw. Not the best way to arrange things if you want to remain sane or to play in octaves!

Sensibly the B and C were changed to give the standard B Draw and C Blow. This still leaves a problem. Logically the next hole should contain D Blow, E Draw. Not only does this mean D Draw first octave, D Blow second octave, it also means (CD) first octave, (DE) second octave.

The present design is a compromise. Make a complete eight note scale unit in four holes (with the change of breath pattern for the B). Make the instrument of three complete scale units. This means that there are two Cs in each octave and when playing the C scale we must jump over one of them.

This is where controversy rears its ugly head and you either have to go with my scheme or someone else's. I believe that 'My' scheme is the same as that used by most of the great players.

The scheme involves one simple rule. Always play C in holes 1, 5 and 9 (and unfortunately in 12). NEVER play C as blow 4. The main reason for this is so that you ALWAYS have the same leap from, say, C to G. You always know that if you are playing a C and then draw you will get a D. This may seem trivial but I think that it is central to a uniform technique. You will find excellent players who argue that your technique should be such that you can handle either 4 or 5 for C. It is up to you to form your own opinion.

The same can be said for the use of E# instead of F in some scales. I favour its use where the result is more musical. Tommy Reilly advocates one way up the chromatic scale and a different way down, for example. I think that it is a good idea and again it is used by many excellent players. Try it and judge for yourself.

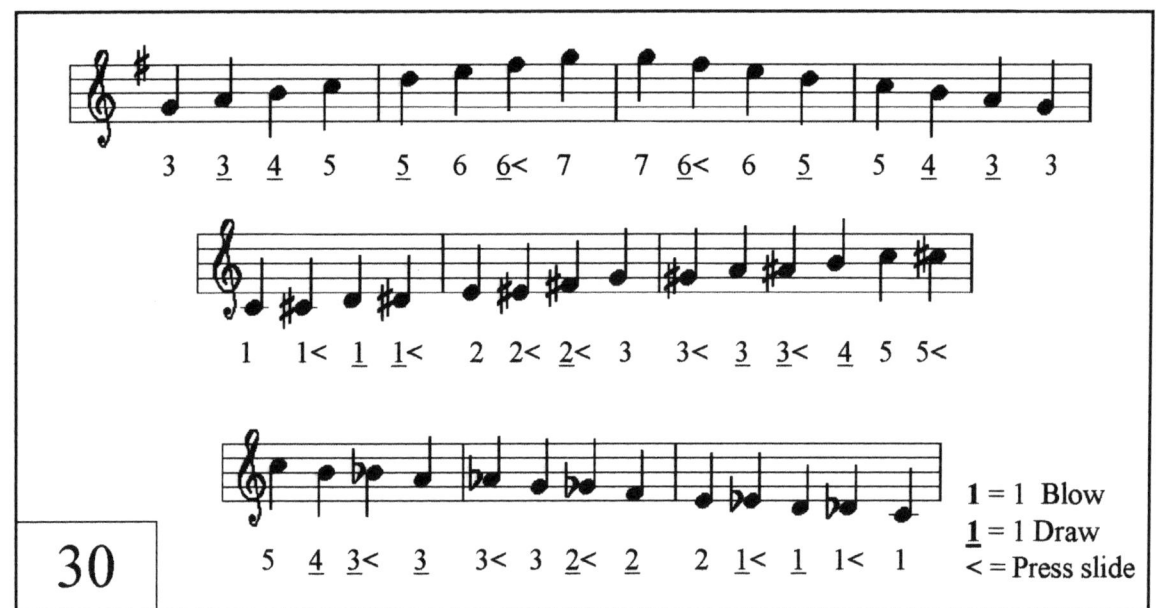

1 = 1 Blow
<u>1</u> = 1 Draw
< = Press slide

Chords and Intervals

You no doubt started off playing the mouth organ being able to play nothing but chords. Controlled chords of 2, 3 or 4 notes are quite easy, but playing separated notes (one on each side of the mouth) is very much more difficult. There is a common technique for playing all intervals but you will find that one interval, for example E2 - C5 with 3 and 4 blocked out, is easiest for you. Experiment to find out which interval is most comfortable for you as follows.

Put your mouth comfortably over the mouthpiece. Blow the several note chord and wiggle your tongue gently onto the instrument until you can hear only the lowest and the highest note of the chord. You should not find this too difficult. Blow and draw making certain that 'extra' notes do not appear when you draw.

Try this width of mouth position a hole up and a hole down. Do the same thing by playing a scale passage up and down a few notes. When you can do this successfully without drowning (wet players will find out what I mean!) you are ready to expand a little. Pupils seem to find it easier to go next to a bigger interval rather than a smaller one. Try the same technique as above with a more stretched mouth position to take in an extra hole. When this is firm, try a passage with this size and then with the original size.

Some people find Octave playing quite difficult and have to really work at it for some time. Do make certain that your mouth position is the same for G - G as for C - C (do not relax a hole on C - C). Now try the three hole interval (C - G). You may have to retract your mouth a little from its normal position. Don't pinch your mouth, try to keep it relaxed - same with the tongue.

The final technique is much more difficult - playing a series of different intervals one after the other, smoothly. This leads to the technique, pioneered by Tommy Reilly in his 'Serenade', of holding a note on the right and playing arpeggios on the left hand side of the mouth at the same time. When this music was first published many players were convinced that it was impossible. Not so! But it does require a considerable amount of work to get it going. One of my favourite professional players admits to not being able to play on the left hand side of the mouth successfully. We can't all do everything.

Tongue switching

A useful technique which comes from Octave playing is the ability to play on the left or the right side of the mouth at will, and to rapidly switch between them. This means that Octave leaps or grace notes at about the octave are easy and very smooth.

Play an octave and then block out the right hand note. Try playing tunes on the left hand side of the mouth. Not only has your tongue expanded to enormous proportions and your tone has disappeared. I have never been able to get the range of volume or tone on the left hand side of my mouth.

When you can do this play alternate passages on left and right, this will help to firm the technique.

To play intervals successfully your harmonica must be very well in tune. Playing single notes most musicians influence a note into tune unconsciously. When playing intervals this is not possible (I don't think) because you cannot subtly alter the pressure and wind speed independently on each side of the mouth. This means that any out of tune notes really show up.

BUT, however well the harmonica is set up some intervals will always sound better than others. This is discussed in another book in this series. (Make your harmonica play well)

Play the Harmonica Well

INTERPRETATION

This is a gigantic subject. I can only touch on some of the essentials in a book of this size.

Whatever type or style of music you are trying to copy or emulate there are many subtle factors which makes it different to any other style. You must know what these are if you are not just going to copy. If you want to advance, or play new music in this style, then you must know its rules and regulations.

Most people can imitate a foreign language and make up sentences which sound as though they really mean something. It only needs a couple of words for a native speaker to realise that you are a complete fake. The same with musical style.

What are these rules? Are they strict rules or flexible? How do you find out about them? Does this apply to 'pop' music as well as 'classical? (Yes it does!) If you study music as an examination subject you will sooner or later be expected to write music ' in the style of Bach ' or Palestrina. You will be expected to recognise Baroque, Romantic, Classical and Modern musical styles. If a 16 year old can do it for GCSE then anyone can given a few basic rules (one of which is .. Listen actively to a lot of different types of music)

There is a big problem with getting a new piece of music and try it out . It is so obvious that most people do not think about it. The fact is that the music you buy is not the music the composer wants you to play! The notes written on the sheet are only a close approximation of what the piece should sound like. The problem is worse when the composer is dead and a few editors have added their ideas as to what the composer meant. Add to this the fact that the ideas people nowadays have of how to play, say, the music of Bach are totally different to the ideas they had in the 1930s (and 1960s!) and you can become very, very confused.

Try playing a piece of music by the Beatles from the sheet music and you will wonder if you have been sold the wrong tune. An example of this is French instrumental music of around Louis XIV time. Notes written as a series of quavers would have been played more like .. dotted quaver, semiquavers .. everybody knew that!

The way to learn style is to listen to recordings and look at the sheet music. What do you look and listen for? Is the sound strictly the same as that shown on the paper? Are the note lengths the same? Are there sudden jumps in volume or are they gradual and subtle? Does 'your' part sound similar to the orchestral parts or does it contrast?

Study the sheet music before you get your instrument out to play.

Look at the Clef Sign. Is it Treble, Bass, Tenor or Alto?
Look at the Key Signature. How many sharps or flats are there? Is it in the Major or Minor key?
Are there any instructions at the start of the piece? Lamentoso, Brightly, Con fuoco.

Play the Harmonica Well

Are there any clues in the Title of the piece? Waltz in Ab, Pizzicato Polka, Dance of Death!
Is there a speed indication? For Metronome, ie crotchet = 100, Allegro con Brio, Slow, Walking pace.
Is there a volume indication? FF, mp, loudly
What is the route map? Are there any repeats, if so where from and to. Are there any indications like Da Capo (DC) of D al Segno? Is the end at the end or somewhere in the middle after going back to the start? As the music almost certainly will not have been written for the harmonica find out what it was written for.

Now is the time to look at the notes. See if you can spot things for the instrument it was written for but not for the harmonica. Be prepared to subtly alter these parts (ie don't necessarily play a set of repeated notes which are there for the syllables of a set of words being sung on a single note).

Are there any technically difficult bits which you need to have a go at separately before tackling the whole thing.?

Now go slowly through the piece observing as many of the points mentioned as possible (AND speed changes AND volume changes AND mood changes etc.). This sounds a long winded process but it is what every musician does with every piece. After a while you will find that it only takes a few seconds .. to start with it takes a little longer!

Repeat sections. In early music repeats sometimes seem a total bore, especially in the slow movements. Don't forget that the approach to music in the past was much more free and 'classical' musicians were expected to do what 'jazz' musicians do today and improvise. The second time through was used to show off the technical skill of the player by improvising on the notes provided by the composer. Strangely, as I write this there is a past master, Michaela Petri (recorder) doing just that on the radio, you could do worse than listen to some of her recordings.

Look at the key signature. Count the number of Sharps or Flats. Look at the table below and you will find that it is one of two keys, a MAJOR one or a MINOR one.

FIND THE KEY

	Flats							Sharps					
	6	5	4	3	2	1	0	1	2	3	4	5	6
Major	Gb	Db	Ab	Eb	Bb	F	C	G	D	A	E	B	F#
Minor	Eb	Bb	F	C	G	D	A	E	B	F#	C#	G#	

Now look at the last note of your tune. This will frequently tell you which of the two keys it is, Major or Minor. Tunes usually end on the name note of their scale, but not always so this method is only a guide.

Play the Harmonica Well

Useful Published Books and Music

This selection of books and music are my own personal choice with no attempt to go outside my own musical preferences. The techniques in this book were developed using these references and a great deal of classical music including much from the Baroque period. Many works by Handel, Bach, Samartini, Vivaldi etc are useful both from the sheer musical value and the physical strength they help to give to all the muscles mentioned above. There are hundreds of thousands of pieces of music, we, unfortunately, do not have enough years to explore it all.

Especially useful or good are shown with a '#' sign.

Books

\# **Oxford Companion to Music** by Percy Scholes
published Oxford University Press

\# **Gramophone Classical Catalogue** (wonderful reference for music, its dates and whether availible or not)

\# **Chambers Pocket Guide to Language of Music**
by Wendy Munro Published by Chambers

What to listen for in Music by Aaron Copland
Published by New American Library

50 Famous Composers by Gervasse Hughes
Published by Pan

\# **Form in Brief** by William Lovelock
\# **Ornaments and Abbreviations** by William Lovelock
Both published by William Elkin
(excellent cheap paperbacks for students)

Introduction to Music by Hugh M Miller
\# **History of Music** by Hugh M Miller
(another pair of excellent paperbacks for students)

A Dictionary of Musical Themes
 by Barlow and Morgenstern
Published by Ben
(Over 10,000 musical themes with easy finding if you can whistle the tune in C !! Wonderful, but quite expensive book)

Music

\# **Country Dance Music albums**
Published by English Folk Dance and Song Society.
(Wonderful folk tunes, well suited to the harmonica and not all that easy!)

Sight Reading Exercises for Descant Recorder
By Philip Rodgers
Published by Schott Edition Schott number 10563
(Fairly boring, but very good progressive exercises)

\# Studies for Oboe by Ferling \# \# \# \#
O.K. I like this one. Marvellous Music. Get It.

Postscript

This is the first in a series of books to be published with the complete harmonica player in mind.

The next three titles will be:

>Play Difficult Music Well
>on the Chromatic Harmonica
>a book of advanced execises

>Make Your Harmonica Work Better
>A book of maintenance, repair and alteration.

>Play Scales, Arpeggios and Chords Well
>on the Chromatic Harmonica.
>Standard scales etc. with specific harmonica 'fingering'

I hope that you have enjoyed this book. More importantly, I hope that you continue to gain benefit from it in the future. We never stop learning.

If you have any ideas for books which are harmonica specific that you would like to see written, please contact me!

Douglas Tate

The revolutionary concepts and innovative design of this distinctive new chromatic harmonica evoke praise from diatonic and chromatic harmonica players alike:

Pat Missin [player and master harmonica technician]:
"I have seen the future of the chromatic harmonica and its name is Renaissance!"

Joseph McIntyre [Renaissance owner]:
"The Renaissance has a sound none of my other chromatics have! It's so smooth and easy to play. Just great!"

Charlie Musselwhite [Renowned blues artist]:
"This is the Rolls-Royce of chromatics!"

Ron Ervin [First Renaissance buyer in the U.S.A.]:
"It slides smoothly in the mouth, but it is SO slick, and it only needs a little moisture! The slider works beautifully!"

Winslow Yerxa [Jazz and blues player; HIP magazine]:
"I haven't tried the ware of all these custom makers, but I have tried the ILUS Renaissance, and I have to say it's the best chromatic harmonic I've ever played... completely redesigned ...powerful sound and amazing response."

Ruth Friscoe [Jazz player and Renaissance owner]:
"I love it, I love it! It plays like a dream... and now I find I don't want to play anything but the Renaissance. I'm spoiled."

Johnny Mars [Popular Blues player]:
"I am falling in love with this instrument... It is incredible!"

George Davis [Classical player]:
"The slide is the smoothest, has the shortest movement of any chromatic I have ever played, and did not leak air! ... a chromatic that really responds to both easy and hard blowing."

Mark Hummel [Wellknown blues player]:
"That's a GREAT chrom!"

Bill Henderson [Classical player and Renaissance owner]:
"I've been playing the 'XXXXXXX' [a top level metal-bodied professional harmonica] for over four years, but this is a real musical instrument at last!"

John Walden [Blues player and Renaissance owner]:
"A superb instrument... Wonderful tone... slide mechanism is almost silent... an absolute delight to play... The Renaissance is an expensive instrument, but... it's worth every penny!"

Ken Deifik [L.A. blues and session player]:
"This instrument represents the maturing of our instrument. The mouth shape is extraordinarily "right". The air leakage one experiences with other chromatics is simply gone. Two harmonicists KNOWING there's a better way... then DOING IT. Serious chromatic players should contact Doug and Bobbie sooner than later. Your playing life will change dramatically."

The Future has arrived...

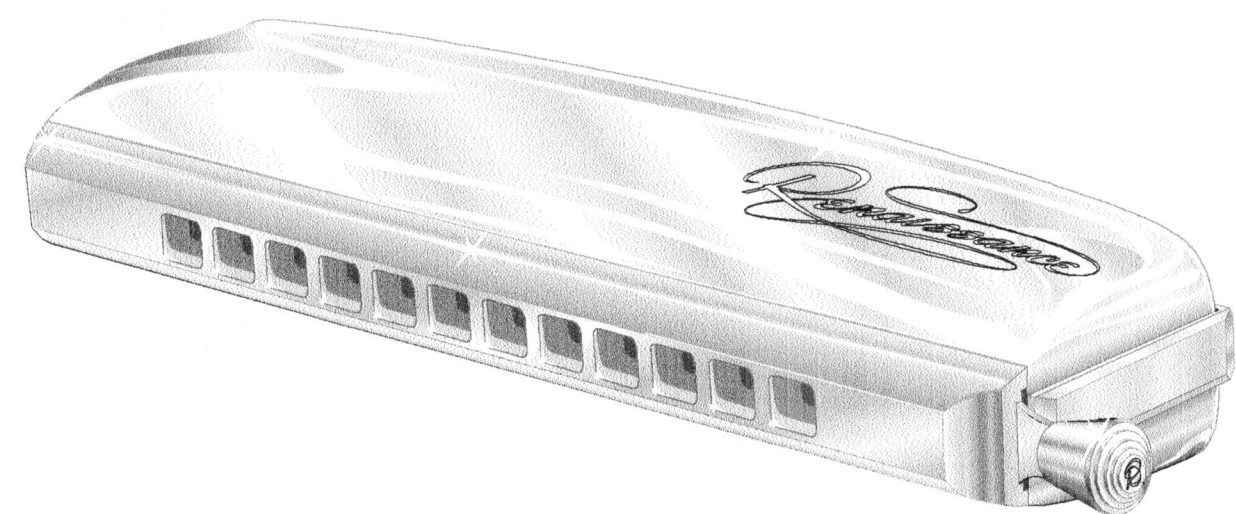

"Renaissance"

◆ The perfect blend of stunning beauty and functional design in a unique new harmonica ◆
◆ Ergonomic design and ingenious engineering add agility and supreme comfort to playing ◆
◆ Exceptionally wide dynamic range and evenness of response allows your musical imagination to fly ◆
◆ Innovative features and practical construction provide for quick and easy maintenance ◆

For more information, contact *ILUS Harmonicas* **at either address shown below:**

 Douglas Tate ◆ 12 Fallowfield, Ampthill, Beds MK45 2TP, United Kingdom ◆ 01525-753-745
dougt_playwell@cableol.co.uk ◀▓ Douglas◆E-Mail E-Mail◆Bobbie ▓▶ bobg@freenet.tlh.fl.us
Bobbie Giordano ◆ 4237 Sherborne Road, Tallahassee, FL, USA 32303 ◆ 850-562-4220

You'll Like What You Hear!

Harmonica Books
from CENTERSTREAM Publications
P. O. Box 17878 Anaheim Hills, CA 92807 - Phone/Fax (714) 779-9390 - E-Mail, Centerstrm @ AOL.com

Bluegrass Harmonica
by Mike Stevens
Extraordinary harpist Mike Stevens has been named Central Canadian Bluegrass Entertainer of the Year five years in a row. In this book, he teaches all the techniques, tips and inside information you need to know to play bluegrass harmonica. He covers: holding the harp, lip pursing, tongue blocking, draw bending, vibrato, attacking the notes, wind chops, and a lot more. The CD features practice tunes for beginning, intermediate and advanced players, including two versions of some of the intermediate and advanced tunes: one at standard tempo, and one slowed down for easier learning.
00000220 Book/CD Pack..............................$19.95

A SOURCEBOOK OF SONNY TERRY LICKS
for Blues Harmonica
by Tom Ball
Centerstream Publishing
Besides 70 famous licks from Sonny, this book/CD pack gives you some quick harmonica lessons, information on Sonny's style, a discography with key chart, and a bibliography for future research. The CD features each lick played out by the author.
00000178 Book/CD Pack..............................$19.95

BLUES HARMONICA – A COMPREHENSIVE CRASH COURSE & OVERVIEW
by Tom Ball
Centerstream Publishing
This new book/cassette pack features a comprehensive crash-course on all aspects of the blues harmonica. Written informally and in only tab notation, this book encourages players to learn at their own pace while developing their own style and feel. The accompanying 32-minute tape includes demonstrations to inspire and aid players in practice.
_____00000159..........................$16.95

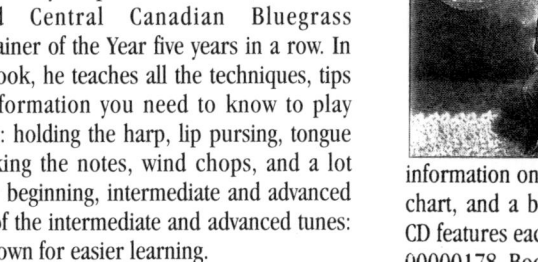

BLUES & ROCK HARMONICA
by Glenn Weiser
Centerstream Publications
Book/cassette package for beginners to learn blues and rock improvisation. Includes explanations of scales, modes, chords & other essential elements of music. The 60-minute cassette features riffs & solos plus demonstrations and a blues jam to play along with.
_____00000127..........................$16.95

Irish and American Fiddle Tunes for Harmonica
by Glenn Weiser
Centerstream Publishing
A complete guide to playing fiddle tunes! Covers: tips on hand positions; playing instructions and techniques; rhythmic patterns for the reel, jig, hornpipe and waltz; and more. Features over 100 songs, along with a CD that demonstrates several of the tunes. Ability to read music is not necessary.
00000232 Book/CD Pack..............................$19.95
(0-931759-10-2)

The Perfect Harmonica Method
by Jerry Perelman
Centerstream Publications
The harmonica opens a wonderful new avenue of musical adventure for classroom learning or individual playing. This book/CD pack is the beginner's guide to learning to enjoy music and play the harmonica. It includes 24 graded lessons with over 65 songs, most of which are demonstrated on the CD. Covers: holding the harmonica, breathing, keeping the beat, playing with vibrato, using eighth notes, playing duets, and more!
00000147 Book/CD Pack..............................$17.95
(0-931759-64-1)

New Books!
Make Your Harmonica Work Better
How to Buy, Maintain and Improve the Harmonica from Beginner to Expert
By Douglas Tate - Foreword by Larry Adler
There is a vast amount of knowledge throughout the world about how to make the harmonica sound and play better, but little of it is written down, that is, until now. This fully illustrated book contains sections on: how to buy a harmonica, common problems, advice about tools with techniques for using them, the basic parts of the chromatic harmonica, solutions which can improve the sound and functionality, experimenting on old harmonicas, tuning, and much more. The musician wants an instrument which doesn't get in the way of his playing, doesn't stick up in quiet passages, has an even response, doesn't let you down when you want that extra decibel of power.
For chromatic players but diatonic harmonica players will learn just as much .   U.S. $ 9.95   HL 00000238   ISBN 1-57424-062-5

Play The Harmonica Well
Advanced Instruction for the Chromatic Harmonica
by Douglas Tate - Foreword by Larry Adler
From beginner to advance, everyone will learn something. The aim is to explain precisely what is required to do in order to achieve the desired skill. Contents include: Holding, Posture, Mouth Position, Movement, Breath Control, Articulation, Phrasing, Tone Manipulation, Vibrato, Trills and Turns, Projection, Chords and Intervals, Interpretation and more. *For chromatic players but diatonic harmonica players will learn just as much.*   U.S. $9.95   HL 00000244   ISBN 1-57424-061-7